CHICK 'n' PUG

For the coolest chicks I know,
Mayzie and Lilia

First published in the United States of America in September 2010
by Bloomsbury Books for Young Readers
www.bloomsburykids.com

For information about permission to reproduce selections from this book, write to
Permissions, Bloomsbury BFYR, 175 Fifth Avenue, New York, New York 10010

Library of Congress Cataloging-in-Publication Data
Sattler, Jennifer Gordon.
Chick 'n' Pug / Jennifer Sattler. – 1st U.S. ed.
p.   cm.
Summary: Chick leaves the boring coop in order to find his hero, Wonder Pug, and a little bit of excitement.
ISBN 978-1-59990-534-1 (hardcover) • ISBN 978-1-59990-535-8 (reinforced)
[1. Roosters–Fiction. 2. Adventure and adventurers–Fiction. 3. Pug–Fiction. 4. Dogs–Fiction.] I. Title. II. Title: Chick and Pug.
PZ7.S24935Chi 2010   [E]–dc22   2010009330

Art created with acrylics and colored pencil
Typeset in Cafeteria and Draftsman Casual
Book design by Nicole Gastonguay

Printed in China by Hung Hing Printing (China) Co., Ltd., Shenzhen, Guangdong
2 4 6 8 10 9 7 5 3 1 (hardcover)
2 4 6 8 10 9 7 5 3 1 (reinforced)

All papers used by Bloomsbury Publishing, Inc., are natural, recyclable products made from wood grown in well-managed forests.
The manufacturing processes conform to the environmental regulations of the country of origin.

CHICK 'n' PUG

Jennifer Sattler

He's BOLD!
He's HANDSOME!
He's . . .

WONDER
PUG!

BLOOMSBURY

NEW YORK BERLIN LONDON

Chick had read *The Adventures of Wonder Pug!* 127 times. Every page was packed with excitement.

But there was no excitement in the chicken coop.

So Chick set off to find some.

It wasn't long before he found a real, live Wonder Pug.

"Wow." Chick swooned. Even asleep he looked wonderful.

Chick waited for his hero to wake up.

HI!

But sometimes, even a hero needs a wake-up call.

"You're Wonder Pug, right?" Chick asked.

"I'm a pug. I **was** a sleeping pug."

"Well, Pug." Chick sighed. "I think you are magnificent. I am going to be a Wonder Pug when I grow up."

"I mean, laying eggs all day?"

"Pecking in the dirt?
What kind of life is that?"

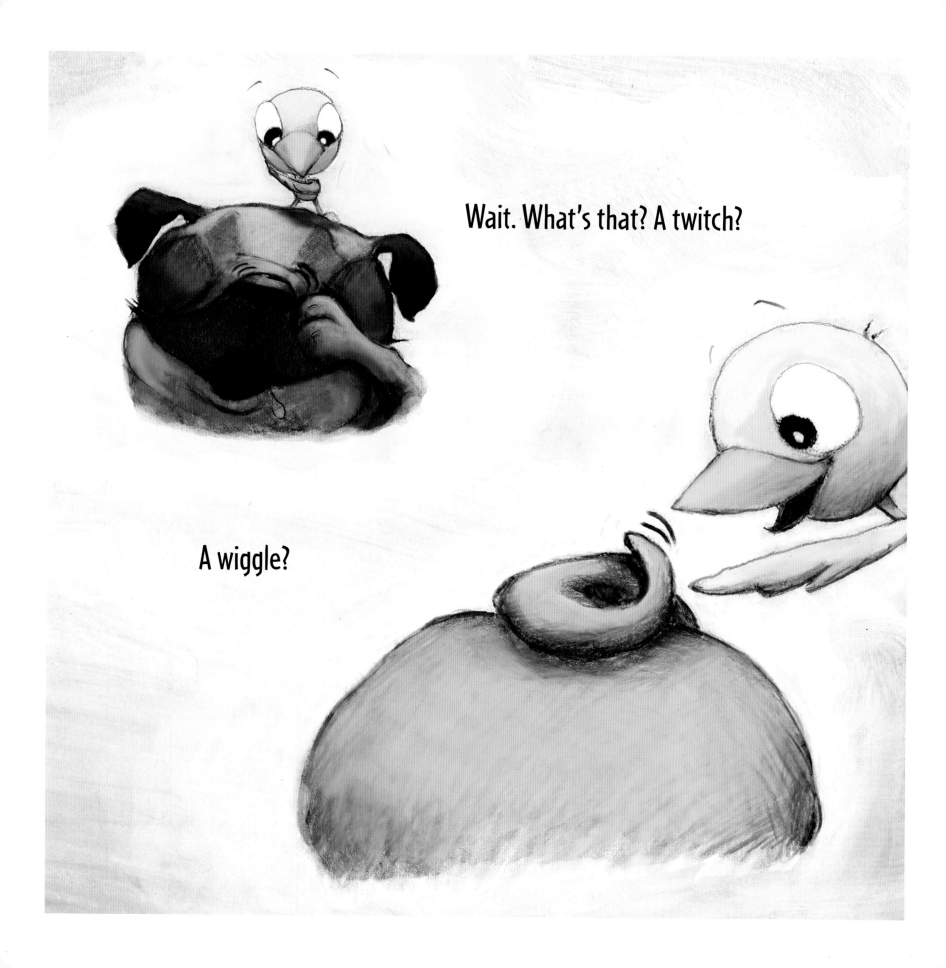

"Okay! Here we go!" Chick was all aflutter
with excitement. "Let the adventure begin!"

"Go get 'em, Tiger! Show that knotted rope who's boss!"

"What about this Frisbee? Are you just gonna let it taunt you like that?"

"You never know when an empty can might turn on you."

"Look at him go! He must have trained vigorously to beat such an opponent!"

Chick was impressed.

"Pug! Pug!

An intruder has entered your territory!"

Clearly, Pug's strategy was to play dead.

"There must be something I can do," thought Chick.

But what? A staring contest?

An egg, right in the kisser?

And then it came to him . . .

Hmmf . . .

"Mr. Snuggles didn't count on Wonder Pug having a sidekick, did he?"